A Visit to the Library

by Rosalyn Clark

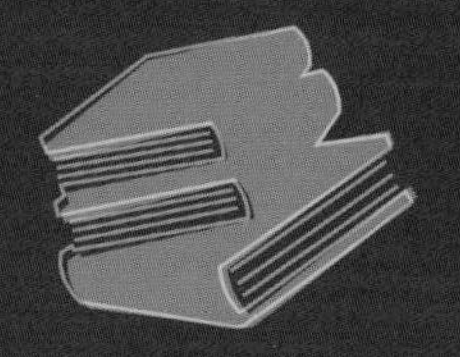

LERNER PUBLICATIONS ◆ MINNEAPOLIS

Note to Educators:

Throughout this book, you'll find critical thinking questions. These can be used to engage young readers in thinking critically about the topic and in using the text and photos to do so.

Lerner Publications Company
A division of Lerner Publishing Group, Inc.
241 First Avenue North
Minneapolis, MN 55401 USA

For reading levels and more information, look up this title at www.lernerbooks.com.

Library of Congress Cataloging-in-Publication Data

The Cataloging-in-Publication Data for *A Visit to the Library* is on file at the Library of Congress.
ISBN 978-1-5124-3374-6 (lib. bdg.)
ISBN 978-1-5124-5562-5 (pbk.)
ISBN 978-1-5124-5044-6 (EB pdf)

Manufactured in the United States of America
1—CG—7/15/17

Table of Contents

Time for a Field Trip

It is time for a field trip!

Today we are visiting

the library.

We meet a librarian.

She shows us around

the library.

Welcome!

A librarian helps us use computers.

We look up where to find books.

What else might you use a computer for at the library?

Each book is on a shelf.

A librarian helps us

find books.

Then it is story time.

A librarian reads a

book aloud.

We listen.

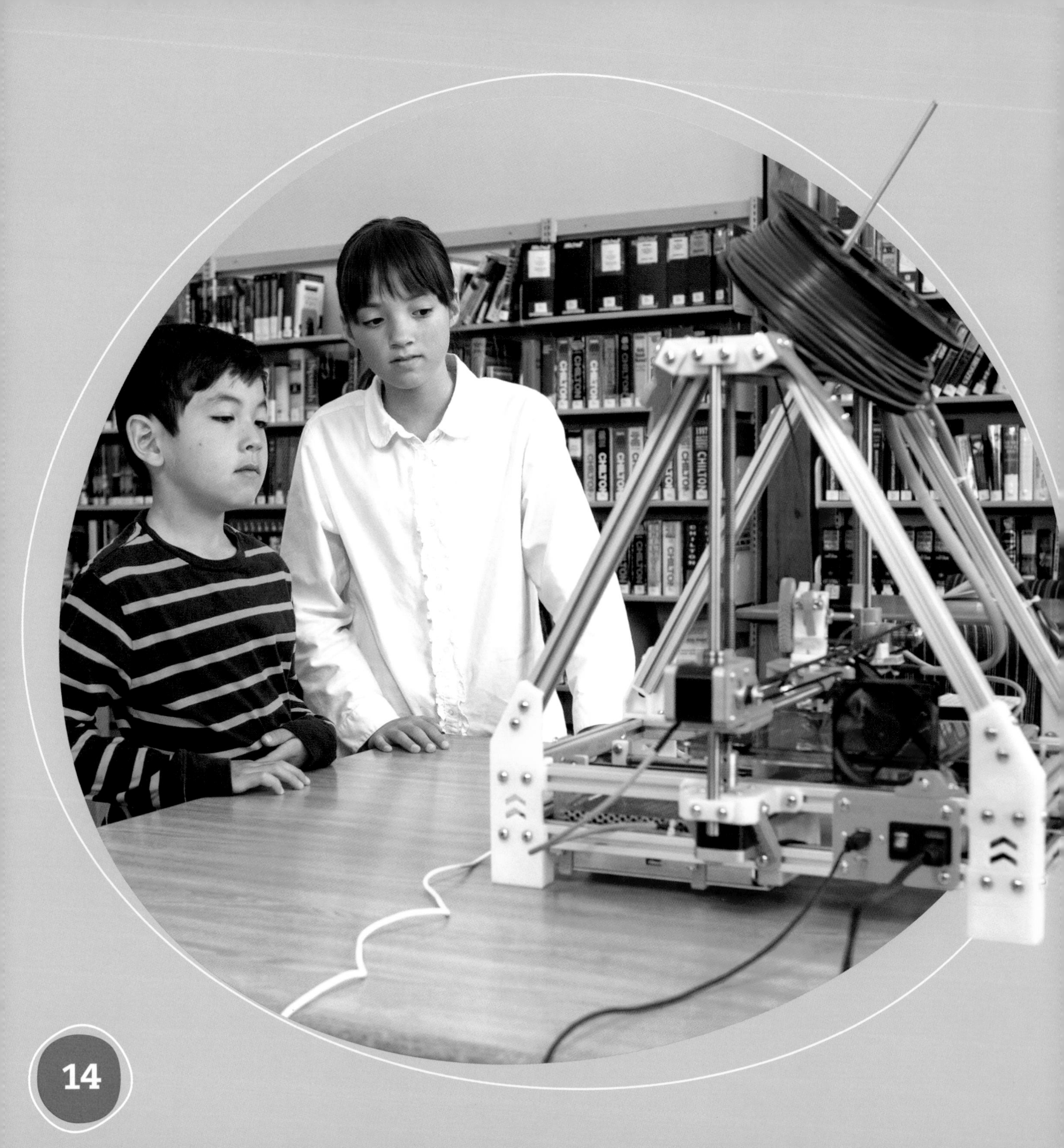
CHILTON

There are many fun things to do

at a library.

The library has 3-D printers.

We print 3-D objects.

What kinds of things could you make with a 3-D printer?

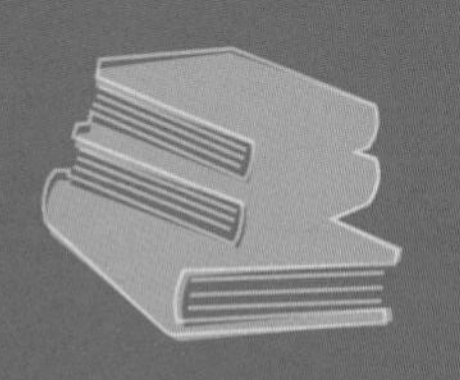

The library also has a robot club.

We can build our own robots.

It is time for us to leave.

We get library cards.

We check out books.

Why do you think people need library cards to check out books?

Add or Subtract
7 2 = 5
CONTINENTS AND OCEANS
CONTINENTS AND OCEANS
THE CHICKEN LIFE CYCLE

There is so much to learn at the library! What would you like to do at your next visit to the library?

What to See at a Library

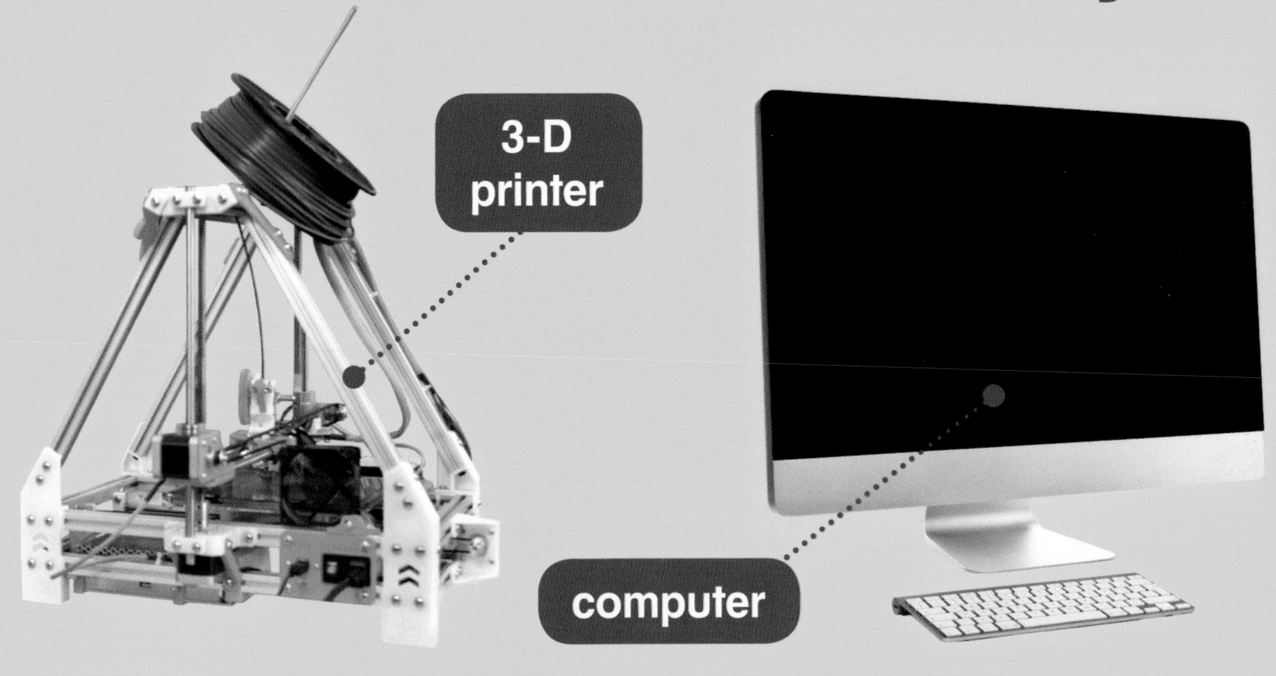

Picture Glossary

computers

electronic machines that store information

library cards

cards library members use to check out books

robot

a machine that is controlled by a computer and can do the work of a person

3-D

three-dimensional, or not flat

Read More

Anderson, Sheila. *Library*. Minneapolis: LernerClassroom, 2008.

Keogh, Josie. *A Trip to the Library*. New York: PowerKids, 2013.

Piehl, Janet. *Explore the Library*. Minneapolis: Lerner Publications, 2014.

Index

Photo Credits

The images in this book are used with the permission of: © Ronnachai Palas/Shutterstock.com, pp. 4–5; © Steve Debenport/iStock.com, pp. 6–7, 17, 18–19, 22 (bottom right), 23 (bottom left), 23 (top right); © wavebreakmedia/Shutterstock.com, pp. 8, 12–13, 23 (top left); © SpeedKingz/Shutterstock.com, pp. 10–11; © Gregory Johnston/Shutterstock.com, pp. 14, 22 (top left), 23 (bottom right); © Rawpixel Ltd/iStock.com, p. 20; © urbanbuzz/Shutterstock.com, p. 22 (bottom left); © Igor Klimov/Shutterstock.com, p. 22 (top right).

Front Cover: © wavebreakmedia/iStock.com/Thinkstock.com.